With a Crash and a B...

Contents

PART 2: Language Arts
The Writing Center

Language, Mechanics, and Usage Lessons

Sentences

Describing Words

PART 1: READING

This Section Provides

- Vocabulary and Skills Support Pages for Major Selections
- Study Skills Pages for *With a Crash and a Bang!*

This Is the Bear

(At this level, some children may need help reading and following directions. Provide support as necessary.)

Decide which word completes each sentence. Print it in the lines.

took   **been**   **fell**

_____

1. I _____ took _____ my friend to see my garden.

smell   **surprised**   **back**

_____

2. She was so _____ surprised _____ !

soon   **well**   **thought**

_____

3. She _____ thought _____ it looked wonderful.

very   **make**   **picked**

_____

4. I was _____ very _____ happy.

man   **knew**   **with**

_____

5. I _____ knew _____ she would like it.

Vowels: Short o

Decide which word completes each sentence. Print it in the lines.

rob　　**fox**　　**fog**

1. A _____fox_____ wants to play a joke.

hot　　**sob**　　**rock**

2. He hides in back of a _____rock_____ .

hop　　**fog**　　**lock**

3. Two rabbits _____hop_____ up to the rock.

socks　　**lots**　　**pops**

4. The fox _____pops_____ out.

top　　**shock**　　**box**

5. What a _____shock_____ to the rabbits!

This Is the Bear

Decide which word completes each
sentence.   Print the word in the lines.

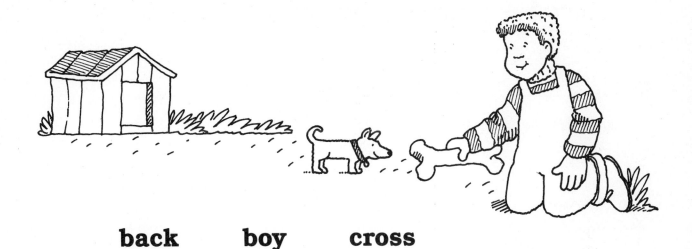

back   **boy**   **cross**

_____

- - - - - - - - - - - -

1. The _____boy_____ gave his dog Pat a bone.

_____

bones   **well**   **pushed**

_____

- - - - - - - - - - - -

2. He knew Pat liked _____bones_____ the best.

_____

him   **home**   **say**

_____

- - - - - - - - - - - -

3. Pat wanted to take the bone _____home_____ .

_____

as   **asked**   **home**

_____

- - - - - - - - - - - -

4. The bone was _____as_____ big as Pat! ⟹

lost   **him**   **never**

5. The boy laughed at _____ him _____ .

need   **boy**   **never**

6. He _____ never _____ thought Pat would do that!

Choose a word from the box to use in a sentence of your own. Tell something about Pat.

home	cold	right

Sample answer: Pat wants to eat right now.

Vowels: Long o

Choose a word from the box to complete each sentence. Print it in the lines. Then read the story to a friend.

rode	home	hopes	nose	stone

1. Max _____rode_____ on his bike.

2. He hit a big _____stone_____ .

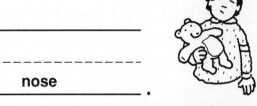

3. Max's bear fell on its _____nose_____ .

4. Max went _____home_____ .

5. He _____hopes_____ Mom can fix his bear.

Reading New Words Strategy

Read the story and answer the questions. Then read the page to a friend. Tell how you figured out the underlined words.

We are <u>going</u> <u>shopping</u> <u>today</u>. We need to get things for our <u>home</u>. Mom and Dad will get <u>pots</u> for <u>cooking</u>. I <u>hope</u> they will get a <u>doll</u> for me, and a <u>bone</u> for our dog!

---

1. Where will the family go today?

Sample answer: They will go to lots of stores.

2. What will Mom and Dad get?

Sample answer: They will buy cooking pots.

Draw what the girl and her dog want.

| child's drawing of a doll | child's drawing of a bone |

Sequence/Character's Feelings

Read the story below.

Baby Bird did not know how to fly. One day, he fell out of the tree.

"What will I do now?" said Baby Bird. "Where is my mother? How will I get back up in the tree?"

"I will help you," said Owl. "Get on my back."

Baby Bird did as Owl said. How that Owl did fly! He went up and up. Soon Baby Bird was back in his tree.

"Thank you, Owl," said Baby Bird.

Owl said, "Here comes your mother. She and I will have a talk. I think it's time to teach you to fly."

Draw three pictures to show what happened first, next, and last in the story.

1.	2.
Child's drawing of Baby Bird falling from tree	Child's drawing of Baby Bird on back of Owl

3.

Child's drawing of Baby Bird in nest

4. How did Baby Bird feel at first?

_____

- -

Sample answers: He was afraid, worried.

_____

5. How did he feel at the end?

_____

- -

Sample answers: He felt safe, thankful.

_____

Vowels: Short/Long o

Decide which word completes each sentence. Print the word in the lines. Then read the story to a friend.

job   **woke**

––––––––––––––

1. Abby has a great new _____ job _____ .

Shone   **Shop**

––––––––––––––

2. She works at the Fix-It _____ Shop _____ .

close   **clock**

––––––––––––––

3. She can fix a _____ clock _____ .

hose   **hot**

––––––––––––––

4. Abby knows how to fix a _____ hose _____ .

hop   **hope**

––––––––––––––

5. I _____ hope _____ she can fix my top.

Base Words and Endings

Read each sentence.   Each underlined word is a base word with an ending.   Circle the ending and print the base word in the lines.

1. Lisa asked me to come to her house.

_____
_ _ _ _ _ _ _ _ _ _ _ _ _
_____ask_____

2. We played with most of her toys.

_____
_ _ _ _ _ _ _ _ _ _ _ _ _
_____toy_____

3. Then we wanted to see who was the fastest runner.

_____
_ _ _ _ _ _ _ _ _ _ _ _ _
_____fast_____

4. We were laughing all day.

_____
_ _ _ _ _ _ _ _ _ _ _ _ _
_____laugh_____

5. I am lucky to have a friend like Lisa.

_____
_ _ _ _ _ _ _ _ _ _ _ _ _
_____luck_____

Compound Words

Print the two words that were put together to make the underlined word in each sentence.

1. Dee loves to sit in her <u>clubhouse</u>.

_____   _____
- - - - - - -   - - - - - - -
club   house
_____   _____

2. She sees <u>blackbirds</u> in the trees.

_____   _____
- - - - - - -   - - - - - - -
black   birds
_____   _____

3. Dee can look over the <u>rooftops</u>.

_____   _____
- - - - - - -   - - - - - - -
roof   tops
_____   _____

4. A <u>horsefly</u> is flying around her.

_____   _____
- - - - - - -   - - - - - - -
horse   fly
_____   _____

5. Soon she must do her <u>homework</u>.

_____   _____
- - - - - - -   - - - - - - -
home   work
_____   _____

Fix-It

Read the story below.

Mom had not finished her work. She called me over. Mom asked if I could please put away my things and watch the baby. I took the baby to her room and put her in bed.

She cried until I found her bear. Then I sang her a song. I tried my best to sing her to sleep. Finally, the baby got sleepy — and so did I!

Print the answers to these questions in the lines. Then talk about your answers with a friend.

1. Why couldn't Mom watch the baby?

_____

Mom had work to do.

_____

2. Where did the boy take the baby?

_____

He took the baby to her room.

_____

3. What did the boy do to get the baby to stop crying?

_____

He gave the baby her bear.

_____

4. What do you think made the boy sleepy?

_____

Sample answer: He worked hard to get the baby to sleep.

_____

_____

Do Like Kyla

Choose a word from the box
to complete each sentence.
Print the word in the lines.
Then read the sentences
to a friend.

1. Rita sees white _____ **snow** _____
   falling outside her window.

stand
snow
page

2. She puts _____ **lots** _____ of
   bread into a big bag.

lots
both
jar

3. Then she pulls on her warm

   red _____ **coat** _____ .

coat
sister
last

4. "I'm going out by myself," Rita

   _____ **says** _____ to her mom.

quick
store
says

5. Rita steps out of her

_____

- - - - - - - - - - - -
_____**front**_____ door.

| page |
| front |
| must |

6. Snow falls on her

_____

- - - - - - - - - - - -
_____**hair**_____ .

| hair |
| only |
| over |

7. Then she runs in the snow

_____

- - - - - - - - - - - -
_____**past**_____ the houses

and trees.

| does |
| end |
| past |

8. Soon she stops and

_____

- - - - - - - - - - - -
_____**sits**_____ in the

snow to rest.

| our |
| way |
| sits |

9. Rita sees many

_____

- - - - - - - - - - - - - - - -

_____**beautiful**_____ birds

in the trees.

10. She knows that the birds can't find any food.   It's

_____

- - - - - - - - - - - - - - - -

_____**under**_____ the snow.

Rita puts bread on top of the snow.   It is for her bird friends. Now they can eat.

Now write more about Rita. Choose a word from the box to use in a sentence of your own.

head	quick	does

_____

- -

_____

- -

_____

Klippity Klop

Decide which word completes each sentence. Print the word in the lines. Then think about what the prince might say. Print it in his speech balloon.

(Answers will vary.)

prince   cave

----

1. A _____prince_____ got on his horse one fine day.

closed   through

----

2. He went for a ride _____through_____ the hills.

fine   field

----

3. Soon he saw a _____field_____ of flowers.

turned   safe

----

4. He _____turned_____ his horse into the field.

rocky   **hill**

5. The field was very _____rocky_____ .

down   **closed**

6. The prince got _____down_____ from his horse.

ran   **safe**

7. He walked slowly to be _____safe_____ .

fine   **down**

8. The prince picked many _____fine_____ flowers.

ran   **hill**

9. Then he rode up a _____hill_____ to get back home.

Vowels: *Short* u

Decide which word from the box completes each sentence. Print the word in the lines.

| mud | suds | pup | sun | tub |

1. Ted called his little _____<u>pup</u>_____ .

2. Its paws had _____<u>mud</u>_____ on them.

3. Ted got water for a big _____<u>tub</u>_____ .

4. He set it in the _____<u>sun</u>_____ .

5. Ted made lots of _____<u>suds</u>_____ .

Use words from the box to complete the sentences.

fun	luck	hug	rub	fuss

_____

6. Ted had to _____rub_____ hard to get the mud off.

_____

7. But Ted was in ____luck____ .

_____

8. His pup didn't make a ____fuss____ .

_____

9. It had ____fun____ in the tub.

_____

10. So Ted gave the pup a ____hug____ .

Vowels: Long u

Decide which word completes each
sentence.   Print the word in the lines.
Then read the story to yourself.

tune   fuse

1. A song is sometimes called a _____tune_____ .

cube   flute

2. Duck played a funny song on his _____flute_____ .

tube   cute

3. The dog thought it was _____cute_____ .

huge   cube

4. And the bear let out a _____huge_____ laugh!

SKILLS SUPPORT
(Language/Decoding)   **21**   **Theme 2   Scared Silly**

Reading New Words Strategy

Read the story below. As you read, circle any words you have to figure out. Write those words in the lines.

Fred the Bunny

Fred is my pet bunny. He likes hopping through the fields. Fred jumps over rocks and runs under bushes. He is faster than most bunnies.

_____

- -

(Words will vary.)

_____

- -

_____

- -

_____

- -

_____

Now read the story with a friend. Talk about how you figured out the words.

Cause-Effect/Reality-Fantasy

Read the story.

Brad had a new, red balloon. He wanted his friend to see it. He looked everywhere for her. As Brad walked through the woods, something went, "Flop, flop. Flop, flop."

The "flop, flop" scared Brad so much that he let go of his balloon. His balloon went up, up in the air.

Then Brad saw his friend, Duck. She hopped onto a rock with a "flop, flop." It was her big, flat feet that went, "Flop, flop," as she walked.

"Oh," cried Brad. "You scared me. I wanted you to see my balloon. But now I've lost it!"

"I will get it back," said Duck. And her wings went, "Flap, flap, flap, flap," as she quickly flew after the balloon.

Now answer these questions about the story.

1. Why was Brad looking for his friend?

_____

He wanted her to see his balloon.

2. Why did Brad let go of his balloon?

_____

He was scared.

3. What happened in this story that really could happen?

_____

Sample answer: A boy could let go of his balloon.

4. What part of the story couldn't really happen?

_____

A duck couldn't talk like a person.

5. Was this a silly or a scary story? Tell why.

_____

Answers will vary.

Vowels: Short u and Long u

Decide which word completes each sentence. Print the word in the lines. Then read the story to a friend.

sun　　**flute**

_____

- - - - - - - - - - - - - - - - - -

1. The _____ sun _____ was out!

mule　　**fun**

- - - - - - - - - - - - - - - - - -

_____

2. All of the animals were having _____ fun _____ .

cub　　**cube**

- - - - - - - - - - - - - - - - - -

_____

3. Mrs. Bear was playing with her _____ cub _____ .

mud　　**tune**

- - - - - - - - - - - - - - - - - -

_____

4. The pigs played in the _____ mud _____ .

rub   tuba

_ _ _ _ _ _ _ _ _ _ _ _ _ _ _ _ _ _ _

5. Mr. Bear played a big _____tuba_____ .

sun   flute

_ _ _ _ _ _ _ _ _ _ _ _ _ _ _ _ _ _ _

6. Fred Fox played his _____flute_____ .

bun   tune

_ _ _ _ _ _ _ _ _ _ _ _ _ _ _ _ _ _ _

7. What a fine _____tune_____ they played!

mule   fun

_ _ _ _ _ _ _ _ _ _ _ _ _ _ _ _ _ _ _

8. Mel the _____mule_____ danced!

CVC Base Words and Endings

Read each sentence below. Circle the ending on the underlined word, and draw a line through the second of the consonants. Then print the base word in the lines. The first one has been done for you.

1. Mr. Yee was di**g**(ging) in his garden.

dig

2. His plants were getting bi**g**(ger) every day.

big

3. He hum**m**(ed) a tune as he worked.

hum

4. Then he saw a fun**n**(y) rabbit race by.

fun

5. It was the fat**t**(est) rabbit Mr. Yee had ever seen.

fat

The Gunnywolf

Read the short story below.

Owl lived in the deep, dark woods. But he liked to fly far away from his home in the trees.

A little girl who lived by the woods went outside to pick flowers. She saw Owl. Owl caught her looking at him. So he looked back. Next he made a funny sound.

Owl's voice surprised the girl. She ran fast. She went back inside her house. Then she felt safe.

Answer the questions about the story.
The underlined words may help you. **(Sample answers)**

1. Where did Owl live? **Owl lived in the deep, dark woods.**

2. What did Owl like to do?

He liked to fly far away from his home in the trees.

3. Where did the little girl live?

The little girl lived by the woods.

4. What surprised the little girl?

Owl's voice surprised her.

5. What did she do after she was surprised?

She ran back inside her house.

6. What would you have done?

(Answers will vary.)

Strange Bumps

Decide which word completes each sentence. Circle the word and then print it in the lines. Read the story to a friend.

off   (own)   were
_____

- - - - - - - - - - - - - -

1. Rags is my _____ own _____ little dog.

same   sat   (by)
_____

- - - - - - - - - - - - - -

2. She likes to sit with me _____ by _____ the fire.

near   (top)   left
_____

- - - - - - - - - - - - - -

3. At night Rags sleeps on _____ top _____ of my blanket.

(while)   fall   sat
_____

- - - - - - - - - - - - - -

4. Rags likes to play _____ while _____ I sleep.

those (**off**) **fall**

5. Last night she pulled my bear and my book

_____

- - - - - - - - - - - - - - - - - -
_____off_____ the bed.

(**moved**) **while** **were**

_____

- - - - - - - - - - - - - - - - -
6. She _____moved_____ them away from my bed.

fire **same** (**those**)

_____

- - - - - - - - - - - - - - - - - -
7. Now she thinks _____those_____ things
are hers!

(**grow**) **moved** **other**

_____

- - - - - - - - - - - - - - - - - -
8. It will be fun to watch Rags _____grow_____ up.

No One Should Have Six Cats!

Circle the word that completes each sentence. Print the word in the lines.

sad   (has)   face

_____

1. Mom _____has_____ a beautiful basket that she made.

(used)   dish   people

_____

2. She has never _____used_____ it.

(old)   keep   else

_____

3. She will give it to an _____old_____ friend.

find   us   (six)

_____

4. Mom put _____six_____ flowers in it.

(**told**)   **bank**   **find**

_____
- - - - - - - - - - - - - - - - - -
5. I _____ told _____ her it would be a great
surprise.

five   **milk**   (**keep**)

_____
- - - - - - - - - - - - - - - - - -
6. Her friend can _____ keep _____ many things
in the basket.

problem   **sad**   (**love**)

_____
- - - - - - - - - - - - - - - - - -
7. I know her friend will _____ love _____
this basket.

people   (**face**)   **which**

8. I can just see the happy look on
_____
- - - - - - - - - - - - - - - - - -
his _____ face _____ .

Vowels: Short e

Decide which word completes each sentence.   Print the word in the lines.

sled   **yet**
_____

1. I can't find my red _____sled_____ .

shed   **went**
_____

2. Did you look in the _____shed_____ ?

stem   **left**
_____

3. Was it _____left_____ by the walk?

vest   **lent**
_____

4. No, I _____lent_____ it to Ben.

get   **west**
_____

5. Well, let's go _____get_____ it, then.

No One Should Have Six Cats!

Read each question. On the line next to each question, print **yes** or **no** for your answer.

1. Are there four children in the picture?   yes

2. Were you first in line today?   yes/no

3. Do bears make better pets than cats?   no

4. Is five more than seven?   no

5. Does it get hot outside in summer?   yes

Write your own questions with **yes** and **no** answers. Try to use words from the box.

| better | instead | first | number |

Ask a friend to print **yes** or **no** for the answers. Have your friend tell why.

1. (Answers will vary.)

2.

Vowels: Long e

Decide which word completes each sentence. Print the word in the lines.

speed   week

1. This _____week_____ we will plant a garden.

seed   deep

2. Each _____seed_____ needs room to grow.

seeks   weeds

3. Who will pull the _____weeds_____ ?

beets   weeps

4. We will have _____beets_____ for dinner.

Use a word from the box in a sentence.

| she   tree   green |

_____

_____

(Answers will vary.)

Reading New Words Strategy

Read the story and answer the questions about it. Then look at the underlined words in the story. Think about how you figured them out. (Sample answers)

We are having a party at six <u>o'clock</u> tonight. Dad <u>baked</u> the bread, and I will <u>cut</u> it. Mom is <u>putting</u> out <u>trays</u> of cheese and <u>nuts</u>. My sister Linda's room is very <u>messy</u>. She needs to pick it up and <u>dust</u> it. She wants me to help.

---

1. When is the family having their party?

They are having their party at six o'clock tonight.

2. What did Dad do to help?

Dad baked bread.

3. What is Mom doing?

Mom is putting out trays of food.

4. What will Linda need to do?

She will need to pick up her room and dust it.

Story Elements/Summarizing

Read the story below.

Andy has a pet frog. His frog loves to jump in the garden.

Andy's sister Kate put the frog outside so she could see him jump. But the frog jumped too far! Kate had a big problem. She couldn't find the frog, and she knew Andy would be angry.

First, Kate looked in the garden. Next, she looked by the trees. Then she looked under five big rocks. Andy's frog was under the last rock!

Answer the questions about the story. Then tell the story to a friend.

(Sample answers)

1. Where did the story happen?

_____

in the garden
_____

2. Who had a problem?

_____

Kate
_____

3. What was the problem?

_____

Kate couldn't find Andy's frog.
_____

4. What did Kate do about the problem?

_____

She looked for the frog.
_____

5. What happened at the end?

_____

Kate found the frog under a rock.
_____

Comparing/Contrasting

Read these stories. Then write about how they are alike and how they are different.

Owls

Owls are birds. They live in trees. Owls go out at night. They look for things to eat. They like to eat rabbits. Some owls even know how to fish.

Little Owl and the Book

It was late at night. Owl was in bed. But he could not sleep. "I will get up," said Owl. "I'll read a book!"

Owl put on his glasses. He found a really good book to read. But then . . .

Owl did not see the sun come up. He was sleeping!

(Sample answers)

_____

- -

They are both about owls. One tells what owls are really like.

_____

_____

- -

The other is a make-believe story.

_____

Contractions

Decide which contraction in each box means the same thing as the two underlined words in the sentence. Write the contraction in the lines.

1. <u>Who</u> <u>is</u> going to win the turtle race?

——————————

Who's

Who's
We'll

2. <u>We</u> <u>are</u> going to see how fast turtles can go.

——————————

We're

Where's
We're

3. That turtle <u>is</u> <u>not</u> moving at all!

——————————

isn't

isn't
I'm

4. <u>They</u> <u>will</u> give a prize to each turtle.

——————————

They'll

There's
They'll

Vowels: Long and Short e

First, read all the sentences. Then print the underlined word from each sentence below the picture that it goes with.

1. On my farm there is a <u>tree</u>.

2. The tree has a <u>bell</u> on it.

3. Under the tree are three <u>sheep</u>.

4. Next to the sheep is a <u>well</u>.

5. In the well are two <u>bees</u>.

_____

bell

_____

tree

_____

sheep

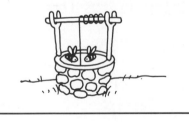

_____

bees

_____

well

Tiger Runs

Circle the word that completes each sentence. Print the word in the lines. Then read about this cat to a friend.

(stay)   **place**   **noise**

1. My cat likes to _____stay_____ outside.

(catch)   **grass**   **such**

2. She tries to _____catch_____ birds, but they fly away.

long   **rain**   (than)

3. My cat is bigger _____than_____ some dogs.

(touch)   **hunt**   **animal**

4. I love to _____touch_____ her soft fur and pet her.

suddenly (before) **than**

_____

- - - - - - - - - - - - - - - -

5. My cat always wakes up _____ before _____ I do.

wind (food) **stay**

_____

- - - - - - - - - - - - - - - -

6. She wants to eat her _____ food _____ .

(meet) **must** **grass**

7. After I feed her, she goes outside to

_____

- - - - - - - - - - - - - - - -

_____ meet _____ her friends.

Now write about cats in your own words.

_____

- -

(Answers will vary.)

_____

- -

_____

- -

_____

Chitina and Her Cat

Decide which word completes
each sentence. Circle the
word and print it in the lines.

(ears)   stars   began

1. Mom gave Tad a rabbit for a pet.

_____

- - - - - - - - - - - - - - - - - -

It had long, black _____ears_____ .

true   (grew)   rounder

_____

- - - - - - - - - - - - - - - - - -

2. Every day the rabbit _____grew_____
bigger and bigger.

began   (box)   louder

3. Tad's rabbit slept in a big

_____

- - - - - - - - - - - - - - - - - -

_____box_____ in the garage.

black   herself   (light)

_____

- - - - - - - - - - - - - - - - - -

4. Tad left a _____light_____ on at night
for his rabbit.

speak ‎(**waiting**)‎ **slowly**

5. And every morning the rabbit was

_____

_____ for him.
waiting

their ‎(**showing**)‎ **waiting**

_____

----

6. As Tad was _____ *showing* _____ his

pet to his friends, it began to shake.

ears **black** ‎(**seemed**)‎

_____

----

7. The rabbit _____ *seemed* _____ afraid

of their loud voices.

‎(**hands**)‎ **brighter** **began**

_____

----

8. Tad picked the rabbit up in his _____ *hands* _____ .

‎(**softly**)‎ **opened** **stood**

_____

----

9. And he spoke _____ *softly* _____ to his

pet so it wouldn't be scared.

ABC Order

Underline the first letter in each word.
Then, in each box number the words
1, 2, 3, 4 to show their ABC order.

<u>r</u>ight __4__	<u>k</u>itten __3__	<u>n</u>eat __2__
<u>h</u>ear __3__	<u>b</u>ump __1__	<u>v</u>oice __4__
<u>a</u>ngry __1__	<u>p</u>urr __4__	<u>s</u>weet __3__
<u>c</u>astle __2__	<u>d</u>ump __2__	<u>g</u>rass __1__

Now look up these words in the glossary
at the back of your reading book. Find out
if you put them in the right order.

Next, look through a book you like to
read. Choose a word you want to know the
meaning for. Print it on this line.

_____

- -

(Answers will vary. First letter should be underlined.)
_____

Underline the letter that would help you
look that word up. Then see if you can find
the word in a glossary or a picture dictionary.

Following Directions

Read the directions. Then follow
them to finish this picture.

1. Draw two windows on the house.

2. Draw a door.

3. Draw a sun shining over the tree.

4. Draw a cloud next to the sun.

5. Color the leaves on the tree green.

Children should finish the picture according to the five-step directions.

Reading Signs

Read the sentences. Print each sentence next to the sign it tells about.

No bike riding here.
You can make a call here.
Don't walk here.

No bike riding here.

Don't walk here.

You can make a call here.

PART 2: LANGUAGE ARTS

This Section Provides

- Writing Center Pages
- Language, Mechanics, and Usage Lessons

WRITING A STORY

Look at the pictures. Draw what happens next.

Children's drawings will vary.

WRITING A STORY

Composition Skill: Beginning, Middle, End

The picture shows the beginning of a story. Draw what happens in the middle of the story. Then draw what happens at the end.

Children's drawings will vary.

Children's drawings will vary.

WRITING A STORY

What was added to this story? Circle
the new words.

(funny)
We saw a ^ show.
(brown)
A ^ bear rode a bike.
(loud)
A seal blew a ^ horn.
(small)
Two ^ dogs rode on a horse.
(four)
Then ^ elephants did a dance.

We had a great time!

WRITING A STORY

Writing Conference

Your name _____

Writer's name _____

1. Does the story have a beginning?

2. Does the story have a middle?

3. Does the story have an end?

WRITING A DESCRIPTION

Our class went to a <u>place</u>.

Our class went to a **zoo**.

Write each sentence. Use an exact word from the Word Box in place of each underlined word.

gray   wolf   teeth   growl

1. We saw a large <u>animal</u>.

We saw a large wolf.

2. It had long, sharp <u>things</u>.

It had long, sharp teeth.

3. Its fur was <u>pretty</u>.

Its fur was gray.

4. It made a loud <u>sound</u>.

It made a loud growl.

THE WRITING CENTER

WRITING A DESCRIPTION
Revising

> ▶ Have I used exact words?

yes ☐

▶ Revise this paragraph. Write exact words in place of each underlined word. Write your changes between the lines.

(Sample answers)

My best toy is a stuffed ~~animal~~. It has
                         tiger
                         ^

~~nice~~ fur and a ~~pretty~~ bow around its neck.
striped   blue

It is as big as ~~this~~. When I hug it, it
               a cat

~~makes a sound~~. I take it with me when
roars

I go ~~places~~. I carry it in my ~~thing~~.
to Grandma's house   backpack

THE WRITING CENTER

WRITING A DESCRIPTION

Writing Conference

Your name _____

Writer's name _____

Are exact words used?

Sentences Make Sense

A **sentence** makes sense.

The words are in order.

For Guided Practice pages, you may want to use the suggestions for modeling that begin on page 81.

us   on   shines   sun   the

(The sun shines on us.)

 Circle the sentences.

jump can frog a

1. (A frog can jump.)

(The grass grows tall.)

3. grows grass the tall

(The fish swim fast.)

2. swim fish fast the

is deep pond the

4. (The pond is deep.)

Copyright © Houghton Mifflin Company. All rights reserved.

LANGUAGE AND USAGE   59

Trace the sentences.

Independent Practice
For Independent Practice pages, read the directions with children and encourage them to complete the page independently.

1. The sun is hot.

2. The pool is cold.

3. The girl is wet.

Sentences Tell

Sentences that tell are **telling sentences**.

 Draw a line under each telling sentence.

1. <u>Mom works.</u>   Mom

2. the tent   <u>The tent is small.</u>

3. <u>A boy finds wood.</u>   A boy

4. sun goes down the   <u>The sun goes down.</u>

5. <u>Mom and Todd camp.</u>   Mom and Todd

Trace the sentences. **Independent Practice**

They tell about the pictures.

1. They sleep well.

2. The sun comes up.

3. Fish swim away.

Writing Capital Letters

A **telling sentence** begins with a
capital letter.

This plant is tall.

 Begin each sentence with the word in
the box.

Begin each sentence with a capital letter.

1. leaves | <u>Leaves</u> are green.

2. birds | Birds eat seeds.

3. roots | Roots are strong.

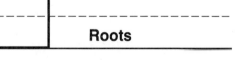

4. plants | Plants grow.

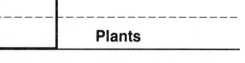

5. people | People eat corn.

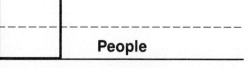

Read the sentences.

 Trace each capital letter. **Independent Practice**

1. ⬛ ad grows flowers.

2. ⬛ is garden is big.

3. ⬛ he children see the flowers.

4. ⬛ va smells the roses.

5. ⬛ he flowers are pretty.

Sentences Ask

Sentences that ask are **asking sentences.**

Circle the asking sentences. Write them.

1. Is that a fish?

2. Can it see?

3. How does it eat?

LANGUAGE AND USAGE

65

✏️ Trace the asking sentences.
They ask about the pictures.

1. How much is it?

2. Can you help?

3. Who called you?

Telling Sentences and Asking Sentences

Telling sentences end with **periods**.

Asking sentences end with **question marks**.

 Circle the telling sentences.

1. Is that a cat?

2. (That is a lion.)

3. Do you have a cat?

4. (I have a dog.)

5. (My dog is small.)

 Draw a line under each asking sentence.

1. Where is the lion?

2. What is it doing?

3. It is sleeping.

4. When does it eat?

5. How old is it?

LANGUAGE AND USAGE

67

Draw a line from each telling sentence to the [.] .

Draw a line from each asking sentence to the [?] .

1. I see a large cat

[.]

[?]

2. What is its name

[.]

[?]

3. Is it a lion

[.]

[?]

4. That is a tiger

[.]

[?]

5. Where does it sleep

[.]

[?]

Writing _I_ in Sentences

Guided Practice

Always write the word **I** as a capital letter.

Lee and **I** like animals.

 Write the word **I** in each sentence.

1. _____I_____ want a pet.

2. _____I_____ will ask Dad.

3. May _____I_____ have a pet?

4. What kind shall _____I_____ get?

 Write a sentence with **I.**

Sample answer: I like big dogs.

Copyright © Houghton Mifflin Company. All rights reserved.

LANGUAGE AND USAGE

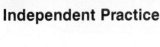 Circle the word **I** in these sentences.

Independent Practice

1. (I) like your green eyes.

2. (I) am your friend.

3. May (I) hold you?

4. (I) can take you home.

5. (I) will call you Shadow.

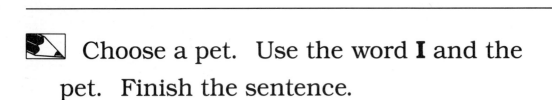 Choose a pet. Use the word **I** and the pet. Finish the sentence.

rabbit   **bird**   **dog**   **cat**

_____

_____

------   ----------------------

__I__ want a pet ___ Answers will vary. ___ .

Guided Practice

I SAILED MY SMALL BLUE BOAT
by Susan A. DeStefano

I sailed my small blue boat
Across a gentle sea.
A quiet summer breeze
Blew it back to me.
Tomorrow when the sun comes up
I will try at least once more
To sail my boat away from me
To a strange and distant shore.

 Write **I** or **me.**   Use the poem to help you.

_____

1. _____I_____ sailed my small blue boat.

2. A breeze blew it back to _____me_____ .

3. _____I_____ will try at least once more.

 Trace **I** or **me**.

Independent Practice

1. I am small.

2. I am round.

3. You hit me with a bat.

4. You catch me .

5. What am I ?

Find out who I am.

Turn the page upside down.

I am a baseball.

Looking and Describing

 Look at the pictures.

Write the words from the boxes that describe what you see.

truck

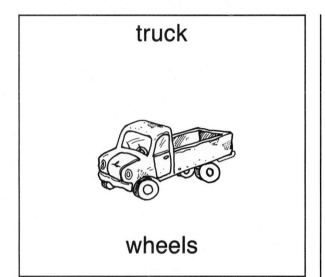

wheels

truck

wheels

old	four
little	

new	eight
big	

1. __old__ truck

4. __new__ truck

2. __little__ truck

5. __big__ truck

3. __four__ wheels

6. __eight__ wheels

LANGUAGE AND USAGE

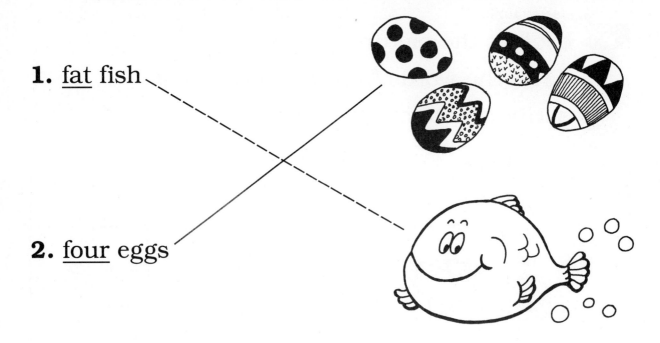

Match the words with the pictures.

Independent Practice

1. <u>fat</u> fish

2. <u>four</u> eggs

3. <u>straight</u> road

4. <u>one</u> egg

5. <u>little</u> mouse

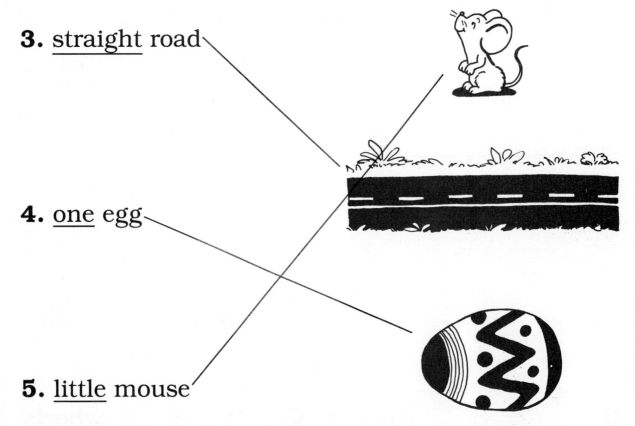

Using Describing Words

Look at the word box. Write the words that describe each picture.

high wall	fast dog	short hair
low wall	slow dog	long hair

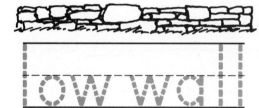

1. low wall

2. slow dog

3. short hair

4. high wall

5. fast dog

6. long hair

Match the pictures with the words.

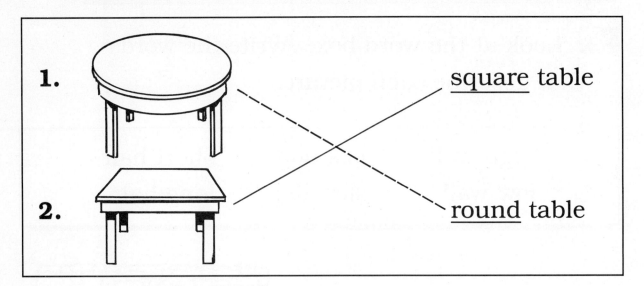

1.

2. square table

round table

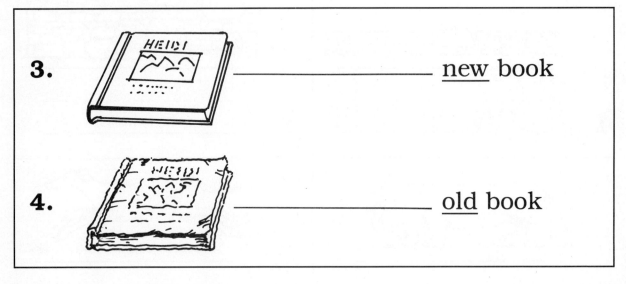

3. new book

4. old book

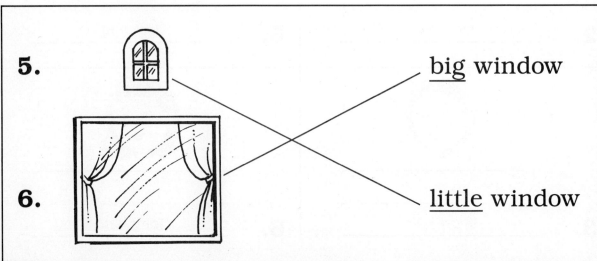

5. big window

6. little window

Describing Words in Sentences

Guided Practice

Describing words tell how things look, taste, smell, sound, and feel.

 Use describing words from the box.
Finish the sentences.

dark clean sweet cold loud

1. The ice feels _cold_.

2. The clothes smell _clean_.

3. The corn tastes _sweet_.

4. I hear a _loud_ bell.

5. The sky is _dark_ tonight.

Trace the describing words.

Independent Practice

1. The waves are ___high___ .

2. The flowers smell ___sweet___ .

3. The bread tastes ___fresh___ .

4. The birds sound ___loud___ .

5. The ball feels ___hard___ .

Overview of Part 1: Reading

SELECTION PAGES

The selection pages provide reinforcement for important aspects of reading the literature in *With a Crash and a Bang!*

How to Use the Selection Pages

Various types of selection pages are referenced at appropriate points in the *Teacher's Book*, as explained below.

Vocabulary pages provide practice for the Additional Support lesson for each selection. These pages include Pretaught and other words that may give some children difficulty. Vocabulary pages are referenced in the Language/Decoding section of the *Teacher's Book* and at the end of the Additional Support lesson.

Skills Support pages provide practice in Comprehension Skills and Language/ Decoding Skills for the Additional Support lessons. These lessons reteach skills taught initially in Developing Strategies and Skills Through Literature.

STUDY SKILLS

Study Skills pages provide independent practice for Additional Support lessons that appear in the Teacher's Handbook at the back of the *Teacher's Book*.

How to Use the Study Skills Pages

Use Study Skills pages when they are referenced at points in the *Teacher's Book* where the particular skill is being used. This may occur in a Teacher's Resources box or an Exploring, Extending, and Sharing activity. The Study Skill page is also listed after the Additional Support lesson.

Overview of Part 2: Language Arts

THE WRITING CENTER

The Writing Center pages of the *Student Resource Book* for *With a Crash and a Bang!* support every Writing Center project presented in the student *Journal*. This Language Arts component of the Reading Program helps children to improve their own writing.

How to Use the Writing Center Pages

You may use Writing Center pages at various points throughout the completion of Writing Center projects. Use them to accomplish the following goals:

- Support and focus children as they work on Writing Center projects.
- Reinforce Composition Skills that apply to different types of writing.
- Teach children to evaluate their own writing and the writing of others.
- Teach children how to revise and improve their own writing.

Suggestions for use of different types of pages are given below.

Composition Skill lessons provide instruction and practice in key skills specific to each type of writing. These skills become the evaluation criteria for children's first drafts and a focus of revisions to their writing projects.

The Composition Skills can be taught as whole-class lessons before children begin a Writing Center project or used as mini-lessons for children having difficulty at any stage of the Writing Process.

Writing Conference pages are a convenient form for children to use in peer conferences. In small groups, children evaluate writing projects in terms of the Composition Skills. Peer conference ideas help the writer revise a writing project more effectively.

A Writing Conference is a peer discussion and evaluation of writing projects. After each writer reads a first draft aloud, the children discuss and evaluate the work. Then the listeners write their comments on Writing Conference sheets for use by the writer in revising the first draft.

Revising pages provide a rehearsal before the revising step of the Writing Process. They remind children how to apply the Composition Skills to a piece of writing. Writers should also be encouraged to revise the content of their writing and improve communication to their readers.

LANGUAGE, MECHANICS, AND USAGE LESSONS

Language, Mechanics, and Usage Lessons have been provided in the *Student Resource Book* for *With a Crash and a Bang!* as an optional resource for teachers who wish to integrate these skills into their reading/language arts curriculum. These lessons provide direct instruction in key language areas: Sentences and Describing Words. Children using *Houghton Mifflin Reading: The Literature Experience* will have a rich variety of reading, writing, listening, and speaking projects and activities. This section provides a useful support for those language arts areas.

These lessons follow the format of those in *Houghton Mifflin English,* but all examples and exercise material are entirely new. Each two-page lesson provides instruction, guided practice, a skill reminder, and independent practice. Suggestions for modeling the Guided Practice part of the lesson can be found on pages 81–83 of this *Student Resource Book, Teacher's Annotated Edition.*

How to Use the Language, Mechanics, and Usage Lessons

Your goals, style of teaching, and classroom organization will guide the use of this section. Because the lessons build sequentially, you may wish to use them in the order presented.

The Language, Mechanics, and Usage Lessons can be used as mini-lessons with small groups or for whole-class instruction. They can also be assigned as independent work to meet individual needs. Some ideas for incorporating the lessons into your teaching are given below.

Option 1: The Language, Mechanics, and Usage Lessons are coordinated with The Writing Center and other activities in the *Journal* for *With a Crash and a Bang!* Annotations for the teacher recommend using *Journal* pages in combination with relevant Language, Mechanics, and Usage Lessons.

Option 2: You might decide to teach all the Language, Mechanics, and Usage Lessons. If so, you may have children complete one section with each of the first two themes in *With a Crash and a Bang!*

Anthology Theme	Language, Mechanics, and Usage Lessons	
First Theme	Sentences	59–72
Second Theme	Describing Words	73–78

Option 3: You might use this section as an additional resource to supplement *Houghton Mifflin English* or another instructional program. Use the book Table of Contents to identify Language, Mechanics, and Usage Lessons for specific skills that present difficulty to individual children in their speaking or writing.

Using the Language, Mechanics, and Usage Lessons

Page 59   Sentences Make Sense

Modeling the Lesson   Display a picture of an object and then describe the object in a sentence with the words out of sequence. For example, show a picture of a ball and say: *round is ball the*. Print these or similar words on the chalkboard and explain that your description doesn't make sense. Then ask children to give you a better description. (For example: *The ball is round.*)

Explain that the group of words they gave you is called a sentence because the words name someone or something and tell what that someone or something is doing. In a sentence, the words must also be in an order that makes sense.

Using the Pupil Page   Help children find page 59. Read the lesson title and definition. Then read the two lines under the top picture. Have children identify the sentence, circle it, and tell why it is correct. (makes sense; the words are in order)

Direct children to the pencil and read the directions aloud. Ask them to look at the picture on the left. Read the two groups of words below it and ask which is a sentence. (second group)

Have a volunteer tell why the second group is correct. (The words are in the right order.) Ask children to circle the sentence in each group.

Page 61   Sentences Tell

Modeling the Lesson   Tape several pictures to the chalkboard, allowing space underneath each one to write one or two short sentences. Point to one picture and call on volunteers to suggest sentences that tell about it. Write the sentences that children dictate under the appropriate picture.

Point out that each sentence tells something about the picture. Explain that this type of sentence is a telling sentence. Call on volunteers to offer telling sentences to answer such questions as *Where do fish swim?* and *What shape is a ball?* Write the sentences on the chalkboard, emphasizing what each one tells.

Using the Pupil Page   Help children find page 61. Read the title and the definition aloud. Then discuss the picture.

Direct children to the pencil and read the directions to them. Read the first two groups of words aloud and ask children to draw a line under the group of words that is a telling sentence. Call on a volunteer to read the telling sentence. Repeat this procedure with the remaining sentences.

Page 63   Writing Capital Letters

Modeling the Lesson   Write these sentences on the chalkboard, placing a box around the initial letters:

T̲his dog runs fast.
I̲t has long ears.

Read the sentences and ask children what they are called. (telling sentences) Point out the boxes around the initial letters and ask children why the boxes are there. (to remind us that a sentence begins with a capital letter)

Using the Pupil Page   Help children find page 63. Read the lesson title and rule. Ask children to look at the picture of the garden and read the sentence beneath it. Ask children to explain the capital *T* in *This*. (begins a sentence)

Direct children to the pencil and read the directions.

The first numbered item has been done. Ask why the answer is correct. (It is capitalized.) Ask children to trace it. Then have children complete the exercise. Provide guidance as needed.

Page 65   Sentences Ask

Modeling the Lesson   Display a picture showing children involved in some activity. Point out one feature and print a telling sentence about it on the chalkboard. Select another feature and make up an asking sentence about it. Write the asking sentence on the chalkboard.

Have volunteers tell how the two sentences are alike and different. (Both are sentences and begin with capital letters. The first is a telling sentence; the second is an asking sentence.)

Have children make up asking sentences and say them aloud. Ask other children to respond with telling sentences.

Using the Pupil Page Help children find page 65. Read the lesson title and definition. Have children study the picture. Explain that the children are at a school science fair and they are asking about what they see. Point out the capital letter and question mark in each sentence in the speech balloons.

Direct children to the pencil. Read the directions and the first asking sentence. Point out the capital letter and question mark. Have children circle the asking sentence and then write it below. Repeat the procedure with the remaining asking sentences.

Page 67 Telling Sentences and Asking Sentences

Modeling the Lesson Print these sentences on the chalkboard.

I like this book.
Why do you like it?
What is it about?
It is a funny book.

Tell children that some of these sentences tell something and some ask something. Ask volunteers to circle the telling sentences. Ask what clue they used to find the telling sentences. (period)

Ask other volunteers to draw a line under the asking sentences. Then ask them what clue they used. (question mark)

Using the Pupil Page Help children find page 67. Read the lesson title and the two rules. Direct children to the first pencil and read the directions. Direct attention to the second item, noting that it has been circled. Ask what shows that it is a telling sentence. (period) Have children trace the circle and complete the exercise. Provide guidance as needed.

Direct children to the second pencil. Read the directions and sentences. Ask a volunteer to tell what clue shows that the first sentence is an asking sentence. (question mark) Have children trace the line and complete the exercise. Provide guidance as needed.

Page 69 Writing *I* in Sentences

Modeling the Lesson Write *ink, pink,* and the lowercase letter *i* on the chalkboard.

Circle each *i* and ask children to identify the letter. Write the capital letter *I* and have children identify it.

Write these sentences on the chalkboard and read them: *Where am I? I am in school.* Point out that when *I* is used as a word, it is always written as a capital letter. Read the sentences again, circling the word *I.*

Ask volunteers to make up sentences telling about themselves. Write the sentences on the chalkboard, circling each capitalized *I.*

Using the Pupil Page Help children find page 69 and read the lesson title aloud. Read children the rule and the example sentence.

Direct children to the first pencil and read the directions aloud. Then read the numbered sentences and have children complete the exercise by themselves.

Direct children to the second pencil and read the directions. Point out the prompt box and ask what belongs inside. (a capital letter) Have children write the sentence.

Page 71 Using *I* and *me* in Sentences

Modeling the Lesson Tell children that they will play an *I/me* game. Begin by asking a child to give you a block or some other small toy.

Say: (Child's name) *gives the block to me.* Then say, as you pass the block to another child: *I give the block to* (new child's name).

Have children pass the block to each other as they repeat the two sentences.

Using the Pupil Page Help children find page 71. Read the lesson title aloud. Read the poem several times. Ask children to try to read it with you.

Direct children to the pencil and read the directions. Tell them that the sentences are mostly from the poem. Read each sentence, allowing time for children to write an answer. Provide guidance as needed.

Page 73 Looking and Describing

Modeling the Lesson Gather several objects from around the room, such as books, a ball, and a box.

Ask children to look at the objects and to tell you the number, color, size, and shape of them. Write their responses on the chalkboard. Explain that these words are describing words that tell about the objects.

Using the Pupil Page Help children find page 73. Read the lesson title, direct children to the pencil, and read the directions. Explain that each picture has three words in a box under it. Each of those words describes or tells about something in the picture. Ask children to listen as you read these words.

Discuss any new vocabulary. Have children trace the first answer and then complete the exercise. Provide guidance as needed.

Page 75   Using Describing Words

Modeling the Lesson Draw a short tree and a tall tree on the chalkboard. Ask a volunteer to put an X on the tall tree. Repeat with a wavy line and a straight line. Ask someone to put an X on the straight line.

Explain to children that the describing words *tall* and *straight* helped them choose the correct pictures.

Using the Pupil Page Help children find page 75. Read the lesson title, direct children to the pencil, and read the directions aloud. Ask children to look at the pairs of words inside the box. Have children identify the pictures.

Point out that the first item has been done. Ask a volunteer to tell why the answer is correct. (*Low* describes the first wall.) Have children trace the answer and then complete the exercise. Provide guidance as needed.

Page 77   Describing Words in Sentences

Modeling the Lesson Write these words on the chalkboard:

sweet   clean   loud   soft
cold   hard   round dark

Then write these sentences on the chalkboard, omitting the words in parentheses:

Orange juice tastes _____. (sweet)
The horns sound _____. (loud)
Ocean water feels _____. (cold)
A wheel has a _____ shape. (round)
The night is _____. (dark)
The fur is very _____. (soft)
My hands are _____. (clean)
The rock is very _____. (hard)

Read each sentence aloud. Ask volunteers to select from the list of words on the chalkboard a word to complete each sentence. Then have volunteers read each completed sentence. Cross out words in the list as they are used.

Using the Pupil Page Help children find page 77. Read the lesson title and rule. Direct children to the pencil. Read the directions and each word in the box. Ask a volunteer to tell why the first answer is correct. (*Cold* describes the feel of ice.)

Read each remaining sentence. Ask children to trace the first answer and then complete the exercise. Provide guidance as needed.